Gorilla Gang

Jean Craighead George

Illustrated by Stacey Schuett

New York

G.G. awoke with a start. He was seven years old, the age when young gorillas, much like human teenagers, gang together for fun and tricks.

This morning G. G., leader of the gang, peered over the edge of his tree nest to see what mischief he could pull off.

He saw Ori, his little sister. She was sleeping in their mother's arms in the next tree nest. "Wraagh," he pestered and showed his white teeth. "Wraagh!"

G. G.'s nasty roar awoke La-Go, the enormous three-hundred-fifty-pound leader of a tribe of twenty-three gorillas of all ages. La-Go opened his soft brown eyes and sat up. His back, neck, and head shone silver-white, for he was a mature gorilla. He was twenty-two years old and the "boss" of the tribe.

He stared at G. G. The prankster stopped wraaghing.

G. G. looked for something else he could do. Il, a twelve-year-old, was sleeping below him in a bed he had built on the ground. Il was a young adult, a blackback gorilla. He was older than G. G. and more dignified.

G. G. broke off a limb and dropped it on him.

Il screamed and jumped out of bed.

La-Go looked to see if Il had been hurt. He had not. The huge silverback belched and glanced from gorilla tree nest to gorilla tree nest. His wives, young adults, and youngsters were waking up in the misty dawn.

G. G.'s mother climbed to the ground. Little Ori clung tightly to her chest.

G. G. broke off a limb. He shook it at Ori.

Pok. Pok. Pok. La-Go was slapping his chest with cupped hands. He frowned at G. G.

G. G. knew what that meant. He stopped pestering Ori.

He looked for something else to do. Ril, a gang member, was still in his nest. G. G. poked his fist through the bottom of it.

"Wraagh. Wraagh. Wraagh," Ril screamed. He swung to the ground. He shook a tree and awoke gang member Lala. She awoke her friend Ri. They all threw grass at each other, then put nose to nose to say hello. They opened their mouths and smiled.

G. G. climbed a tree and sat on a limb. "Hoo, hoo, hoo." His hoots were not very loud. *Pok. Pok. Pok.* He beat his chest first with one cupped hand then the other. His poks were not very loud. When La-Go beat his chest he could be heard for a mile.

Disappointed with his noise, G. G. dropped to the ground and sat with his back to Lala. He lifted up his arms to say in gorilla talk, "I want to be groomed." Lala combed the leaves and grass from his fur with her long nimble fingers. Then she turned her back and G. G. groomed her.

G. G. stood up. La-Go was leading the tribe to breakfast. G. G. hooted, then led his gang to breakfast, smashing trees as he went.

The gorilla tribe moved slowly. In a whole day they would not wander more than four hundred yards.

After a short hike La-Go sat down to crispy celery shoots. The gang sat down, too.

G. G. was stuffing down a juicy stalk when he saw his mother hugging Ori.

"Wraagh," he yelled. Ori was frightened. She cried.

G. G. was pleased. His voice was big enough to scare Ori.

G. G. smelled a sweet musky scent. Another gorilla tribe was passing unseen among the jungle trees.

La-Go knuckled his way to a fallen tree. He stood on it, strutted, and swelled out his chest. His hair stood up all over his body. He turned sideways to show the enemy his powerful sway-back. He was a terrible sight. The strangers walked faster.

La-Go gave three sharp barks. "Who are you?" he asked them.

There was no reply.

"Hoo hoo hoo." La-Go yelled twenty times. No answer. *Pok. Pok. Pok.* He beat his chest with cupped hand a hundred times. No answer.

G. G. studied La-Go. The big silverback gorilla was everything he would like to be. He was big, powerful, noisy. But he never did battle. He didn't have to.

The strange tribe disappeared. The forest was quiet.

Around ten o'clock that morning the gorillas stopped eating. It was nap time. Mothers nursed their babies. Oldsters slept. Youngsters chuckled and played.

G. G. broke off a tree limb and beat the ground to annoy Ori. Ril grabbed it and chased G. G. They hooted and knocked down trees.

La-Go ignored them. He leaned back against a tree trunk and burped long and gloriously.

Ori climbed her father's big belly to his head. She played with his ears. She twisted his eyebrows. La-Go liked babies. Especially this one. He took her gently in his arms.

G. G. wraaghed in jealousy. He ran up a tree until it bent under his weight and carried him to the ground. He somersaulted down the mountain. He broke sticks. Ril and Lala chuckled and followed him.

In the late afternoon G. G. saw little Ori climb a sennecio tree. He waited until she was quite high, then suddenly ran beneath her.

"Hoo. Hoo. Hoo," he yelled.

Startled, Ori let go. She fell.

She tumbled down through the limbs, wailing for her mother. A crotch stopped her fall.

She landed with an "uggh." But Ori could not move. She was stuck.

G. G.'s mother hooted and climbed swiftly to her baby. She shook the tree to dislodge her. She only wedged Ori deeper into the crotch.

The other females screamed. La-Go roared and barked. The blackbacks thundered. Ori was in terrible trouble.

G. G. looked at his sister. She was choking. Her chin was caught in the crotch. She was hanging by her head. Her arms were flailing.

G. G. climbed to her.

Ori whimpered pitifully.

G. G. climbed closer.

She threw her flailing arms around him.

The baby's arms felt good.

G. G. kept right on climbing and Ori kept right on hugging, until, by chance, G. G. lifted her right out of the crotch.

His mother took her baby and hugged her lovingly.

G. G. hung from the tree crotch by one arm. He beat his chest triumphantly.

POK. POK. POK. His voice was louder than it ever had been. He looked at his father.

La-Go gave him the twinkle eye, the look of gorilla approval. He strode off to eat in the blackberry patch. The tribe followed. G. G. did not hoot and smash trees this time. He followed quietly.

The gorillas stuffed themselves for hours.

"Baaaaaaaaaaaaaaaaaaap," belched G. G. "Ori is an okay baby," said his long belch.

If La-Go loved Ori, then he did, too.

Gorilla Talk

in posture and sound

I'M DANGEROUS.
Pok. Pok. Pok.
Repeated many times by slapping the chest. Also a growl.

WOULD YOU GROOM ME?
Hands and arms up.
Back to friend.

GET GOING, YOU RIVAL.
(Silverbacks only)
Rise on hind legs, throw vegetation into the air, kick one leg in the air; run sideways. Thump on ground with palms.

BABY TO MOM.
Crying and temper tantrums. Wails and cries when left alone. Chuckles when happy.

YOU'RE WONDERFUL.
Embracing. Social grooming.

FACIAL EXPRESSIONS

LET'S PLAY.
Open mouth, smiling, eyes relaxed.

WATCH OUT. I'M BOSS.
Strutting walk, sway-back, head turned away, but sneaking looks. Arms bowed out at elbows. Hair bristling.

I'M AFRAID.
Open mouth, brow raised. Eyes shifting nervously. Head slightly back.

NUTS TO YOU.
"Wraagh" with teeth showing.

HELLO.
Nose-to-nose greeting.

Can you find the names of the gorillas in this story in the letters of their scientific name, *Gorilla gorilla*?

Disney is committed to wildlife conservation worldwide. At Disney's Animal Kingdom, most of the animals that guests will see were born in zoological parks. A safari adventure ride features live animals in a re-creation of the African savanna. Guests can also visit Conservation Station, the headquarters for conservation and species survival activities.

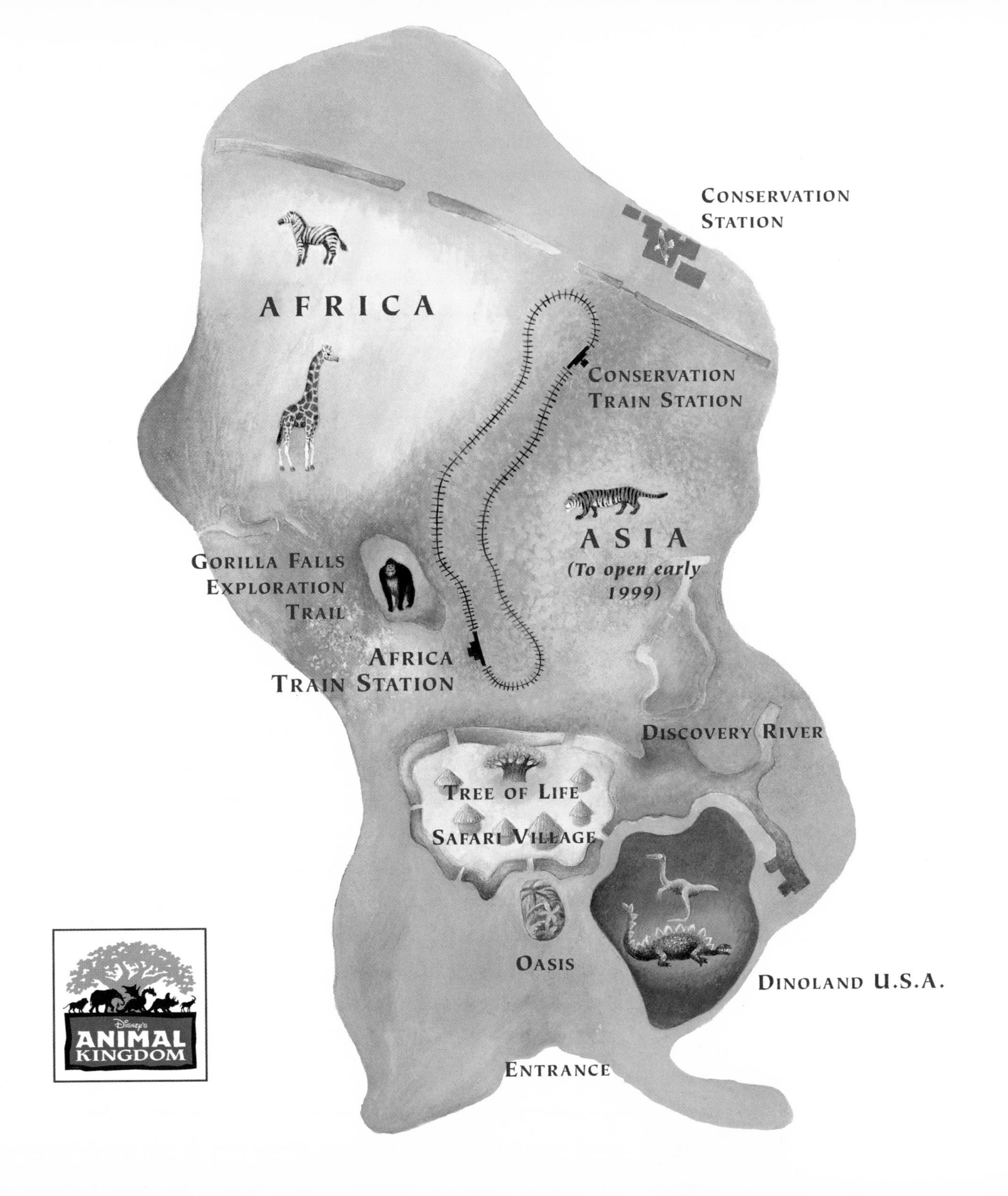
Conservation
Station
Africa
Conservation
Train Station
Asia
(To open early
1999)
Gorilla Falls
Exploration
Trail
Africa
Train Station
Discovery River
Tree of Life
Safari Village
Oasis
Dinoland U.S.A.
Disney's
Animal
Kingdom
Entrance

To Tyler—J.C.G.

To Riley, with love—S. S.

Printed in the United States of America.

First Edition

1 3 5 7 9 10 8 6 4 2

The artwork for each picture is prepared using watercolors.
This book is set in 16-point Tiepolo Bold.
Designed by Stephanie Bart-Horvath.
Library of Congress Catalog Card Number: 98-87730
ISBN 0-7868-3166-9